SUSAN AND JAMES PATTERSON

Illustrated by
HSINPING PAN

CUDDLY CRITTERS for little GENIUSES

jimmy patterson

JIMMY Patterson Books
Little, Brown and Company
New York Boston London

Scarlet Macaw

This smart bird can imitate words and do tricks, and even knows its shapes and colors! The scarlet macaw can live up to eighty years.

Roseate Spoonbill

Eating pink algae turns the roseate spoonbill's feathers pink,
like cotton candy with red peppermint stripes! It has a flat
spoon-shaped bill that helps it dig for food.

Royal Flycatcher

The royal flycatcher has spectacular plumage, or feathers, on its head that looks like a brightly colored fan. It can build a nest up to six feet long.

Sunset Moth

This colorful insect is often mistaken for a butterfly. Its dreamy, shimmering wings have made it an inspiration for jewelry and other art.

Toucan

The toucan makes funny noises with its colorful bill.
It sounds like a cross between a pig and a frog!
Its heavy bill and short wings mean it's not the best flyer.

Sugar Glider

This tree dweller rarely ever touches
the ground. With parachute-like
webbing between their arms and legs,
sugar gliders can
glide as far as half
a football field!

Snowy Owl

Like its name suggests, the snowy owl can live in very cold places, with temperatures as low as forty degrees below zero. It's such a fast and powerful flyer that it can knock down a grown man!

Lovebird

One of the smallest kinds of parrot,
the lovebird got its name because
it stays with one mate for life.
After being separated, lovebirds
will feed each other to
show their love.

Potoo

This bird can hide in plain sight.
It looks like a tree branch when it sits still.
Even potoo chicks hardly move.
Their white baby feathers make
them look like tree fungus.

Sunda Colugo

Living only in trees, the Sunda colugo
can leap so far between branches that it seems
to be flying. When it's scared, it climbs
up, up, up to the top of a tree
to escape any trouble.

SWIMMERS

Irrawaddy Dolphin

These playful creatures speak to one another
by making clicking, creaking, and buzzing sounds.
Irrawaddy dolphins always look like they have
big smiles on their faces!

Hooded Seal

When the hooded seal gets scared or excited,
its nose blows up like a big red balloon.
So it looks like a clown!

Blanket Octopus

With wide webbing between its arms, the blanket octopus can look scary to its enemies. Females can grow to more than six feet, but males are only about an inch long!

Parrotfish

From its birdlike beak, it's easy to see how the parrotfish got its name! At night, it produces a special cocoon over its skin so predators can't smell it while it sleeps.

Dumbo Octopus

Unlike other octopuses, the adorable dumbo octopus lives so deep in the ocean that it doesn't need to squirt ink to hide itself, because the water is already dark.

Blobfish

The blobfish looks like a normal fish at the bottom of the sea where the water is heavier, but its soft bones and skin droop into blobs when it comes up to the surface.

Blue Dragon

Look but don't touch!
The blue dragon is a sea slug
that can float upside down.
It's small and beautiful
but also tough—it gives
a painful sting!

Axolotl

Also called a walking fish, the axolotl is
a salamander with feathery gills that let
it breathe underwater. With its cute face
and ageless smile, it's adorable.

Angel Shark

With a head as flat as a pancake, the angel shark
waits near the floor of the ocean for prey to swim
above, then launches up quickly to catch dinner.

Puffer Fish

To scare off enemies,
the puffer fish can swallow
a lot of water to blow
itself up like a balloon.
It can puff up to more
than double its normal size!

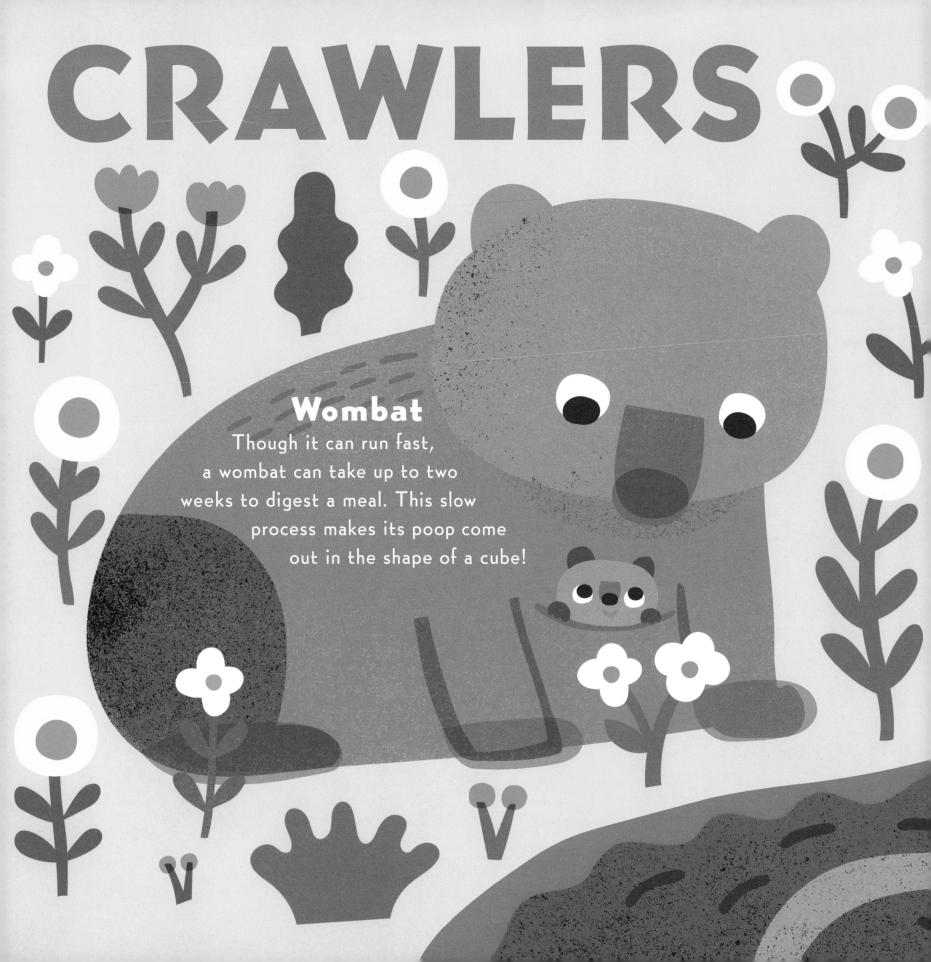

CRAWLERS

Wombat

Though it can run fast,
a wombat can take up to two
weeks to digest a meal. This slow
process makes its poop come
out in the shape of a cube!

Hedgehog

Even though it's small, the hedgehog is very fast—it can run six feet per second! This shy creature is covered in seven thousand sharp quills that keep nosy neighbors away.

Angora Rabbit

Underneath that soft and fluffy mop of fur is the Angora rabbit. It needs to eat a lot of hay to help digest the fur it accidentally swallows while grooming itself. Oops!

Badger

Fierce and powerful, the mighty badger can force larger animals away with sheer toughness. Thick and loose skin makes this mean, clean digging machine almost impossible to hurt. Go Badgers!

Margay

It may look like a cat, but the margay
will never get stuck in a tree—
it can crawl down headfirst
thanks to its flexible ankles.
It's also very strong—
it can hang from a branch
by one paw!

Tree Kangaroo

With its strong legs, the tree
kangaroo can jump to the ground
from a branch six stories high!
It keeps cool in the summertime
by licking the fur on its arms.

Tarsier

This critter has a funny face! Each of the tarsier's huge eyes is heavier than its whole brain. It can also rotate its head 180 degrees, like an owl.

Tonkin Monkey

When Tonkin monkeys talk to one another, they sound like they're hiccuping! These rare animals love to groom each other and pick bugs out of their friends' fur.

Ploughshare Tortoise

Because the bamboo forests they live in are disappearing, ploughshare tortoises are endangered, which means there are only a few left living in the wild.

Blue Poison Dart Frog

Beware of the cute little frog that's no bigger than a paper clip! Kiss this frog and you'll get sick.

Aye-Aye

The silly-looking aye-aye
has big ears that help it
listen for bugs crawling inside trees.
Then it uses its very long middle fingers
to poke into holes to get the
bugs out and eat them!

Tapir

On hot days, the tapir loves to swim to cool off.
It can hold its breath for a few minutes underwater.
If it wants to stay down longer, it uses
its snout as a snorkel.

Red Panda

The red panda uses its large, bushy tail as a blanket to keep warm in the cold mountains, and to help keep its balance when climbing trees.

Markhor

With its long, curved horns, the markhor goat can scratch its own back. That's relaxing! It has excellent climbing skills to quickly scale mountains and escape enemies.

Maned Wolf

When in danger, the maned wolf
puffs out the black fur on its back to look bigger
and scarier. It smells so bad that its
nickname is the skunk wolf.

Gerenuk

This antelope has a very long neck—
like a giraffe's! It stands on its
hind legs to reach high branches
and never has to drink water
because it eats so many leaves.

Dik-Dik

The little dik-dik's funny name comes from the whistling noise it makes when it's scared. It can do a neat trick—whistle with its nose!

Bongo

This antelope has horns that each have one and a half twists. It likes to take mud baths to stay cool on hot, muggy days. And its name sure is fun to say—BONGO!

Southern Red Muntjac

The southern red muntjac is a small deer, but it bravely wrestles with bigger animals using its antlers. It also barks just like a dog.

Pangolin

The only mammal in the world that's covered in scales is called the pangolin.
It can eat up to twenty thousand ants a day. Yum.

Echidna

The echidna looks like it's made from parts of many
different animals. Like porcupine spines.
A bird beak. And a kangaroo's tummy pouch.
It has an extra-long claw on its second toe
to groom its super-spiky spines.

Fennec Fox

Though it may be the smallest fox in the world, the fennec fox has gigantic ears! Their big size helps the fox hear prey underground and also keeps it cool in the hot desert where it lives.

Chinchilla

It has the softest fur and the sharpest teeth around. The chirpy chinchilla can jump six feet high. But watch out— it might pee on you if it gets scared. It also likes to eat its own poop.

Pink Fairy Armadillo

The pink fairy armadillo is so good at digging with its big claws that it seems to swim through the ground! It curls up inside its shell to stay safe.

Panther Chameleon

Thousands of kaleidoscopic crystals on the
panther chameleon's skin let it blend
in and hide. Its tongue is twenty-six times
longer than its body, and its eyes can move
in different directions.

Panda Ant

Bet you can guess how the panda ant got its name!
It looks like a panda, right? But it's a wasp that can
tip a cow over with its nasty sting.

Jerboa

What looks like
a mix of a mouse and
a kangaroo? An adorable
little jerboa! It can jump almost
seven feet in the air and run
crazy fast in zigzags.

Aardwolf

To mark its territory, the aardwolf creates a
musky juice while clucking and barking to
keep unwanted guests away. With its long,
sticky tongue, it can eat thousands
of termites in one lick.

For Susan, my talented and very funny bride, the love of my life. — J. P.

For Jim, my talented and very funny husband, the love of my life. — S. P.

For Mom and Dad: Thank you for your unconditional love and support. I love you! — H. P.

ABOUT THIS BOOK

This book was edited by Jenny Bak and designed by Gail Doobinin with art direction by Tracy Shaw. The production was supervised by Lisa Ferris.
The text was set in Bernhard Gothic and illustrations were created using Adobe Illustrator and Photoshop.

Text copyright © 2018 by James Patterson and Susan Patterson / Illustrations copyright © 2018 by Hachette Book Group, Inc. / Illustrations by Hsinping Pan

JIMMY Patterson Books / Little, Brown and Company / Hachette Book Group / 1290 Avenue of the Americas, New York, NY 10104 / JimmyPatterson.org
First Edition: August 2018
JIMMY Patterson Books is an imprint of Little, Brown and Company, a division of Hachette Book Group, Inc. The Little, Brown name and logo are trademarks of Hachette Book Group, Inc.
The JIMMY Patterson Books® name and logo are trademarks of JBP Business, LLC.
The publisher is not responsible for websites (or their content) that are not owned by the publisher.
The Hachette Speakers Bureau provides a wide range of authors for speaking events. To find out more, go to hachettespeakersbureau.com or call (866) 376-6591.
ISBN 978-0-316-48628-6 / LCCN 2018941167
10 9 8 7 6 5 4 3 2 1
IM / Printed in Italy